The
Bathwater Gang

The Bathwater Gang

by Jerry Spinelli

Illustrated by Meredith Johnson

1837

Little, Brown and Company

Boston   New York   London

First Edition

The characters and events in this book are fictitious.
Any similarity to real persons, living or dead, is
coincidental and not intended by the author.

Library of Congress Cataloging-in-Publication Data

Spinelli, Jerry.
    The bathwater gang/by Jerry Spinelli; illustrated by Mere-
dith Johnson.
        p.   cm.
    Summary: Bertie's all-girl gang becomes involved in a harm-
less but heartfelt war with an all-boy gang, until Bertie's grandmother steps in with a perfect solution.
    ISBN 0-316-80779-6
    [1. Gangs — Fiction.   2. Grandmothers — Fiction.]
I. Johnson, Meredith, ill.   II. Title.
PZ7.S75663Bat   1990
[E] — dc20   89-13318
                                                  CIP
                                                   AC

10

COM-MO

Printed in the United States of America

For my own Bathwater Gang:
Kevin
Barbara
Jeffrey
Molly
Sean
Ben

1

Bertie Kidd was bored.

And it was only the second day of summer vacation. Not to mention only nine o'clock in the morning of the second day.

"I'm bored," she whispered.

"I'm *bored*," she said.

"I AM BORED!" she shouted.

No one heard her. Her mother and dad had gone to work.

She came downstairs and looked at the rocking chair by the front window. It was empty, as usual.

When Granny had come to live with them, Mom and Dad had bought the rocking chair and placed it by the front window. This seemed perfectly normal. After all, that's what grandmothers do, isn't it? They sit in rocking chairs by front windows.

Hah! Somebody forgot to tell that to Bertie's grandmother.

She called: "Gran-neeee!"

No answer.

Where was a grandmother when you needed one?

Bertie grabbed her skateboard and went outside. She stood at the corner of Oriole and Elm and looked in all directions. No Granny in sight.

She started rolling. Ten minutes later, way up on Buttonwood Street, she spotted something bright pink in the distance. It had to be either her grandmother or a flamingo.

Bertie pushed off. Her skateboard wheels clacked over the sidewalk cracks.

"Gran-neee!" she called. "Gran-nee!"

Granny waved, but she didn't stop. She was "wogging." That was her word. It meant faster than a walk and slower than a jog.

Of course, there was no such thing as a wogging suit, so Granny had had to settle for a jogging suit. It was the brightest pink she could find. "So people can see me coming," she explained. Granny loved attention.

As usual, several little kids were wogging along with her. Among kids, Granny was the most popular person in the West End. It wasn't just Bertie who called her Granny. They all did.

Bertie pulled alongside. "Granny, wait up. I have to tell you something."

"I can't wait up," said Granny. "I can't stop when I'm wogging."

"Granny, I have a problem."

Granny lifted her knees higher. "I feel like I could run all day. I feel like I could jump

over that roof. I feel —" she threw her arms in the air — "splendiferous!"

"Gran*neee!*" screeched Bertie. "I'm bored!"

"Nice to meet you. I'm Granny."

"Granny, you're not funny." She picked up her skateboard. She had to trot to keep up. "There's nothing to do, and there's eighty-one days of summer vacation left, and I'm bored already. At this rate I'll be dead of boredom by July."

They arrived at a corner. Cars were coming. In order to keep moving, Granny wogged in a little circle. Bertie stood in the middle.

Granny said, "You miss school."

"I do not," Bertie protested.

"Don't interrupt," said Granny. "You miss school. You miss all the kids. You're a people person. You need to be around people."

"So?"

"So," said Granny, crossing the street as the last car passed, "start up a gang."

Bertie stayed on the sidewalk, letting her grandmother's words sink in.

Gang.

Sure! That's it!

"Thanks, Granny!" she called.

Granny waved. She was already halfway up the next block.

Bertie hopped on her board and took off down the Elm Street hill. She knew exactly who her first gang member would be.

2

Bertie skateboarded straight to the house of Damaris Pickwell, her best friend. Bertie could not imagine having a gang without Damaris.

Sure enough, Damaris was thrilled.

"A gang! Wow! Yeah! Great idea!" And then she said what she usually said when a new idea came up: "I'll ask my mom."

"Damaris," whined Bertie, "what's there to ask? All you're doing is joining a gang. It's not like we'll be robbing a bank or anything."

9

"Only take a sec," said Damaris, hurrying off to telephone her mother at work.

This always annoyed Bertie, Damaris's running off to ask permission. Bertie liked to just *do* things.

When Damaris returned, the answer was all over her face. "I can't," she said.

"Why not?" asked Bertie.

"My mom says gangs aren't good. She says one gang leads to another, and trouble starts."

"Did you tell her it was *my* gang?"

"She said all gangs are that way."

Bertie wanted to scream. Many years before, Mrs. Pickwell had been a flower child. As Bertie understood it, this meant she went around in long dresses and bare feet, tossing rose petals everywhere and saying "Love" to everyone she met.

Flower children were very big on Peace. Mrs. Pickwell was still that way. Even in this day and age, she could sometimes be seen with a blossom in her hair.

"Damaris," said Bertie, "I don't mean to say anything bad about your mom, but sometimes she carries this peace business a little too far."

"My mom hates war."

"Da-*mar*-is. We're not starting a *war*. We're starting a *gang*."

Damaris shrugged. "Well, I'm sorry. She said no."

Bertie kicked a table leg. "Yeah, great. And she never would have said no if you hadn't asked her."

"Don't kick our furniture."

Bertie gave another kick. "Gonna stop me?"

Damaris's face got red. She stomped her foot. "See that, Bertie Kidd? You don't get your way, and you start acting like a baby."

"*You're* the baby." Bertie smirked. "Always asking *mommy's* permission."

"A little obedience never hurt anybody. Maybe you should try it sometime."

"Well, maybe *you* should try finding some new friends. Because you're going to be the only one around who's *not* in the gang."

Damaris stood tall. "I'll survive." She walked to the door and held it open. "You may leave now."

As Bertie passed by, she did not look at Damaris. But she did mutter: "Banana nose."

"What did you call me?" said Damaris.

Bertie stopped and turned and repeated very clearly: "Ba-na-na nooooze."

Damaris sniffed. "Sticks and stones may break my bones —"

"Blah blah blah," said Bertie. "Watermelon head."

Damaris's lip quivered. "Well . . . pumpkin face."

"Goose face!"

"Turkey feet!"

Bertie leaned into Damaris's face. She bared her teeth. She snarled, "Boogie breath."

Damaris's lower lip flapped. Before she could slam the door shut, she was bawling.

Bertie bounced up the sidewalk. As usual, when she and Damaris had a fight, Damaris had been the first to cry. Bertie punched the air with her fist. "Victory!"

So why didn't she feel so good?

3

It always happened that way. Bertie would win the fight. Then Damaris would cry. Then Bertie would feel rotten.

What was the use of winning?

This was as rotten as Bertie had felt in her whole life. She thought of something Granny often told her: When you're down, look up.

She looked up. All she saw was the sky. Granny said if you kept looking up long enough, you'd see something good.

So Bertie kept looking up — and walked

into a fire hydrant. She tumbled to the side-walk. "Phooey!" she growled.

But when she picked herself up, a good thing happened. She got an idea: I'll have a *good* gang. I'll have the best gang there ever was! Then Mrs. Pickwell will have to let Damaris join.

Off she went to find members for her gang.

She tried Jenny Johnson's house. A neighbor said Jenny was away on vacation with her parents.

Andrea Miller had the chicken pox.

Grace Bondi said she would never join a gang that included her worst enemy, Kathy Hobbs.

Kathy Hobbs said she would never join a gang that included her worst enemy, Grace Bondi.

Nancy Keen, who wanted to become a ballerina, said belonging to a gang might damage her toes.

Helen Jenkins said she would join only if she could be captain. Bertie withdrew the invitation.

Joy Lin was too old.

Erin Bohannon was too young.

As a last resort, Bertie knocked for Tiffany Hongosh. Tiffany lived next door. Even though she was the same age as Bertie, she acted like a big-deal, fancy-pantsy movie-star lady.

Sure enough, when Tiffany answered the door, she was wearing lipstick, eye makeup, and big hoop earrings. To Bertie, she looked like a clown.

Bertie swallowed hard and forced the words out. "Want to join my gang?"

Tiffany's snooty nose got even snootier. "*Gang? Me?*" She laughed. "Don't be silly. I don't have time for such childishness. I have too many other activities."

"Oh, yeah? Like what?" Bertie asked, pok-

ing Tiffany in the chest. "Hair curling? Toe-nail clipping? *Nose picking?*"

Tiffany turned green and gasped. She slammed the door shut.

Bertie couldn't think of anything mean enough to yell at Tiffany, so she just gave the door a kick and left.

Bertie wandered over to her backyard. Except for making Tiffany turn green, the day had been a bust. Not a single member for her gang so far.

She could think of only two others to ask.

She hated to do it. It was embarrassing to think that these two were the only two she could get.

On the other hand, she knew they would not say no.

4

After dinner Bertie found Granny in the basement, throwing darts.

"Aren't you supposed to be knitting in a rocking chair or something?" Bertie kidded.

"I'm saving that stuff for when I get old," said Granny. "How's the gang coming?"

Bertie slumped onto the bottom basement step. "Terrible. I had a fight with Damaris. She's not allowed to join. Nobody joined, except two."

"Two?" said Granny. "That's not terrible. That's terrific."

"I made them join," said Bertie. "It was too embarrassing to say nobody joined."

"Do I know them?" asked Granny.

"Well, sort of," said Bertie.

"So, who are they?"

"Clara and Wilma!" blurted Bertie, and she began to cry.

Granny burst out laughing. Clara was Bertie's pet hermit crab. Wilma was a fat worm that lived in the petunia patch out back.

"I'm sorry," sniffed Granny, wiping her eyes. "I didn't mean to laugh when you were crying. It's just the idea of Clara and Wilma in your gang."

Bertie wiped her eyes, too. "Well, now you know why I'm so miserable."

"Yep," Granny agreed. "Now I know. Move over."

Granny sat on the step beside Bertie.

Granny knew when to kid around with Bertie and when to be serious. Bertie hardly ever cried. And she never cried in front of anyone but Granny.

She put her arm around Bertie. "Rotten day, huh?"

"Totally." Bertie sniffled.

"Okay," said Granny. "Let me think a minute."

Granny got up and started throwing darts at the dart board. She did some of her best thinking while throwing darts.

Suddenly she turned. "Teasers!"

"Teasers?" echoed Bertie.

"Right. It means if you want people to join something, you offer them something in return."

"Like what?" asked Bertie.

"Well," said Granny, "it could be anything." She thought some more. "Look at the navy. They don't just say 'Join the navy.' They say, 'Join the navy and see the world.' "

Bertie slapped the step. "Yeah. Okay. Gotcha!" She ran up the stairs.

Five minutes later she was back. She showed Granny a poster she had made. It said:

JOIN BERTIE'S GANG
AND SEE
THE
WORLD!!!!

For the second time, Granny burst out laughing.

5

"I sure am cracking you up tonight," said Bertie.

"I know, I know." Granny chuckled. "And you're not even trying."

Bertie looked at her poster. "So what's so funny? It's a teaser, isn't it? If it's good enough for the navy —"

"Your teaser," said Granny, "has to be truthful. You can't offer something you can't deliver."

"Oh," said Bertie.

She ran back upstairs.

"Daddy," she said, "I want kids to join my gang. What can I offer as a teaser?"

"A million dollars," said her father.

"Thanks, Dad. You're a real big help."

She asked her mother, who said, "Well, what do kids like?"

"Pizza!" piped Bertie.

"There you are," said her mother.

That night Bertie got out her crayons and made five posters. They said:

WANT FREE
PIZZA?
JOIN BERTIE'S
GANG

Then to each one she added a final line:

NO BOYS!

Early next morning, even before Granny went wogging, Bertie was outside. She tacked the posters onto five telephone poles up and down Oriole Street.

She set up her office next to the front steps: a card table, a chair, a sign-up sheet, and a pencil. She waited for the recruits to come pouring in.

The first to show up was Andy Boyer. He had one of the posters in his hand. He did not look too happy.

He threw the poster onto the card table. "What's this stuff?" he demanded.

"What's it *look* like?" Bertie growled back. "I'm starting a gang."

He pointed to the last line. "I mean *this* stuff."

"Want me to read it to you?" sneered Bertie. "It says NO BOYS. Okay? NO . . . BOYS."

"You can't do that," said Andy.

"I can do anything I want," said Bertie. "It's my gang."

"My mom says it's against the law." Andy's mom worked for a lawyer. "You can't keep somebody out because they're from a different sex. That's dis-crim-in-a-tion."

Bertie snatched back her poster. "Listen, buster. I already signed up a worm and a hermit crab. I'm not going any lower than that. Now take a hike."

Andy jabbed a finger at Bertie's face. "I'll take a hike — but I'll be back."

6

Before long, Andy was back, with a poster of his own. It was mounted on a stick. One side said:

BERTIE KIDD
UNFAIR
TO BOYS

The other side said:

DO NOT
JOIN
HER GANG

Holding the poster high, he marched back and forth in front of Bertie's house.

"Get off my property," said Bertie, "or I'll call the cops."

Andy took one step into the street. "Now I'm not on your precious property. And I have a right to freedom of expression. It's in the Constitution." He grinned and went on marching.

Soon girls began to arrive. A few of them became frightened and left when they saw Andy picketing.

But most of the girls walked right on past him and put their names on the sign-up sheet.

They came from all over the neighborhood.

They came from all over Two Mills.

They even came from Bridgeport, the town across the river.

Their names filled three sign-up sheets. There were fifty-nine of them.

"Ya-hoo!" shouted Bertie. "This is more than a gang. It's an army!"

She dashed inside. She whipped off a poster, tacked it to a broom handle, and took it outside. She waved it in Andy Boyer's face. It said:

HAH-HAH!

At dinnertime, Bertie told everyone of her great success.

"Fifty-nine!" marveled Granny. "Pizza sure is a powerful teaser."

Her father asked, "When is the pizza party?"

"Saturday," said Bertie.

"And who is paying for all this pizza?" asked her mother.

"Uh-oh," said Bertie.

As planned, a pizza party took place in Bertie Kidd's backyard on Saturday. All fifty-nine girls showed up.

Dee-Dee Pizza delivered ten large pizzas. Bertie paid the man. It cost her her next twenty weeks of allowance. Plus all of her leftover birthday money. Plus three hours of work that she owed her mother.

But it was worth it. Fifty-nine kids in her backyard — and she the boss of them all!

Bertie told everyone that the first meeting of the gang would be Monday morning at ten o'clock.

For the next two nights, Bertie could hardly sleep. She kept seeing herself as the leader of fifty-nine people. Fifty-nine girls saluting her. Fifty-nine girls calling, "Hail, Captain Kidd!"

Monday morning at ten o'clock, two girls showed up.

7

_____

"Only *two?*" squealed Bertie.

The two who had shown up were Amy Moss and Liz Caputo.

The three of them looked up and down the streets.

They waited until ten-thirty.

They waited until eleven o'clock.

Nobody else showed up, except Granny. "Well," she said, "it looks as if the others were more interested in pizza than in gangs."

34

"It's not fair," grumped Bertie. "They should pay me back for the pizza."

"Look at it this way," said Granny, putting her arms around Amy and Liz. "It's better to have two you can count on than fifty-nine you can't count on."

"I know," Bertie agreed. "But I thought I could count on Damaris. I want her to join, too."

"I'll tell you what," said Granny. "I'll trade you some advice for a ride on your skateboard."

"Skateboard? Granny, you're too —"

Granny's finger pressed Bertie's lips. "Ah-*ah*. Don't say it."

"Sorry, Granny," said Bertie. "You can use the skateboard. What's the advice?"

"Okay," said Granny. "Now, the key here is to impress Damaris's mother, right?"

"Right."

"She thinks gangs are bad, right?"

"Right."

"So you want to show her *your* gang is good, right?"

"Right."

"So —" Granny stepped onto the skateboard. She rolled a few feet. "Hey, this is easy!"

"Gran-*neee*," said Bertie. "So what do we do?"

"Write a platform," said Granny.

"A *platform*? What's that?"

"It's a list of things you believe in. The things your gang stands for."

Granny pushed off on the skateboard. "Show it to Mrs. Pickwellllllllll . . ." she called as she sailed down the sidewalk.

Bertie and Amy and Liz sat down at Bertie's kitchen table with pencils and paper. Here is what they wrote:

OUR GANG PLATFORM

36

This is what we believe in.
We stand for these things too.
1. God
2. parents
3. grandparents
4. great-grandparents
5. great-great-grandparents
6. great-great-great-grandparents
7. uncles
8. aunts
9. pizza (extra cheese)
10. soda
11. birthday parties
12. birthday cake
13. birthday presents
14. Christmas presents
15. Easter presents
16. Fourth of July presents
17. Groundhog Day presents
18. Peace
19. Love
20. Flowers

Bertie added the last three especially for Damaris's mother.

"Okay," she said, "let's show Mrs. Pickwell our platform."

The three girls headed for Mrs. Pickwell's thrift shop. They took the shortcut through the alley between Oriole and Chain Streets.

They had gone only a short way when suddenly someone jumped out from behind a garage door. It was Andy Boyer.

He stood in front of them, hands on hips, a sneer on his lips. "Where do you think you're going?"

"To Marshall Street," said Bertie. "Now, move."

"You're not going this way," said Andy.

"No?" said Bertie. "Why not?"

"Because this is our territory."

Bertie looked around. "*Whose* territory?"

"Ours." Andy grinned. "I have a gang now, too. All boys. This alley is our territory — and you're in it."

8

Bertie poked Andy in the chest. "I've been coming down this alley all my life, and I'm not gonna stop now. Especially not for you. Out of our way, armpit breath."

Much to her surprise, Andy stepped aside. "As you wish." He even bowed.

"Where's your law now, hairball?" Bertie smirked.

Andy merely smiled.

Bertie, Amy, and Liz started walking — and found out why Andy was smiling. From the roofs of two garages, Andy's gang — Itchy Mills and Noodles Overmeyer — began pelting them with water balloons.

Within moments, the girls were soaking wet. The platform was a soggy, blurry mess in Bertie's hand.

Andy's gang was racing away, leaving only their laughter behind.

Bertie shook her fist. "Okay, Boyer! You asked for it! THIS IS WAR!"

And war it was.

Bertie, Amy, and Liz returned to their homes and changed into dry clothes. Then they met in Bertie's bedroom. They planned their first move.

That evening, while Andy Boyer was having dinner, they let the air out of his bicycle tires. Then they poured molasses over the seat.

When Bertie awoke next morning and looked out the window, she found the backyard covered with clothespins.

And so it went, day after day.

Bertie's gang left a chocolate cupcake with white icing on Noodles Overmeyer's front steps. They rang the doorbell and hid behind a car to watch. They knew he would eat it. Noodles ate everything.

Noodles did come out. And he did eat it — until he realized that the white icing was shaving cream.

Andy's gang ambushed Amy Moss on her way to the dentist. They grabbed her by the leg and pulled off one of her sneakers. Then they flung it into Finsterwald's backyard, from which no kid had ever returned alive.

Bertie's gang pelted Andy Boyer's front door with eggs.

Andy's gang pelted Bertie with eggs.

Bertie's gang, by mistake, pelted Andy's father with eggs.

*   *   *

The war raged on.

Every time Bertie saw her best friend, Damaris Pickwell, she thought of what Damaris's mother had said: *One gang leads to another . . . and trouble starts.*

It looked as if Mrs. Pickwell had been right. And that meant Damaris would never be allowed to join.

But Bertie had no time to worry about that. She was too busy with the war.

And then one day it started to rain.

9

Boy, did it rain . . . and rain . . . and rain . . .

The gangs stayed indoors. It was too wet to go to war.

When the rain finally stopped, everyone's mind was on one thing.

"Mud!" shouted Bertie's gang.

"Mud!" shouted Andy's gang.

Kids raced to their rooms and changed into their bathing suits. Then they raced to the dead end of Oriole Street . . . across the tracks . . . across the path to the park . . . to the place known as the Mud Hole.

To the kids of the West End, mud was summer snow.

The best thing about the Mud Hole was that it was at the bottom of Mud Hill. One slide down Mud Hill, and you were hooked forever.

By the time the gangs showed up, kids were already zooming down the hill.

Some slid down on plastic snow coasters, some on trash-can covers, some on cookie pans.

One kid came down hanging ten on a surfboard. And some sailed down on nothing but the backsides of their bathing suits.

Even the Pickwells' pet duck, Roscoe, came down. His webbed, orange feet made perfect mud skis.

There was mud wooshing and mud squooshing . . . mud flopping and mud slopping . . . mud races and mud faces.

Then someone shouted: "Mudball fight!"

There were no sides. Everyone was so covered in mud, no one could tell who was who. So everybody flung mudballs at everybody else.

When the party began to break up, one of the mud creatures called, in Damaris Pickwell's voice: "Oriole and Chain Street kids, follow me! Ducks too!"

A dozen kids marched up Rako Hill and into the Pickwells' backyard. They were one motley, happy mob of mud-o-maniacs.

Damaris turned on the garden hose. She squirted herself from head to toe till all the goo was gone.

Then she aimed the hose at Roscoe, and Roscoe became a white duck again.

Then she began hosing down the others. One by one, as though the hose were painting them, kids appeared. Familiar faces. Familiar problems.

Two of the mud creatures were having a laughing time finger-painting each other's backs. Then the hose hit them, and they discovered who they were: Bertie Kidd and Andy Boyer. The laughing turned to name-calling.

Two others were tickling each other when the hose water arrived. They turned out to be Amy Moss and Itchy Mills.

They were two gangs again — insulting and mocking each other. Once again, war was on their minds.

Suddenly, someone called out: "Look!"

Everyone looked.

Damaris was hosing off the final mud creature. The hose began at the creature's feet and moved upward. By the time it reached the waist, it was clear that the body belonged to no kid anybody could recognize.

Finally the face appeared from under the mud.

Everyone gasped: *"Granny!"*

10

Granny was all wet and shiny in her yellow bathing suit.

"Granny!" said Bertie. "What are you doing here?"

"What's it look like?" said Granny. "Getting my mud washed off."

"You were at the Mud Hole?"

Granny grinned. "You think I'm gonna let you kids have all the fun?"

Granny's grin disappeared. "At least, I *was* having fun. Till you guys —"

The two gangs — three boys and three girls — were off and fighting again. Shoving. Snarling. Shouting.

But not louder than Granny shouted: "SHUT UP!"

Six shouters shut up.

Granny lowered her voice but spoke sternly. "Look at you. A disgrace. A bunch of hoodlums. You were nicer when you were covered with mud." She shook her head sadly. "There's only one thing left for me to do."

She started to walk away.

"What?" the kids called. "What?"

Granny stopped. She turned slowly. She gave a smug little smile. "I'm starting my own gang."

She walked away.

The kids just stood there.

It took about ten seconds for Granny's words to sink in.

It took another ten seconds to decide that she was serious.

It took one second to realize this was the chance of a lifetime.

And it took no time at all for the six of them to catch up to her.

"Granny, I'll join!"

"Sign me up, Granny!"

"Me, Granny!"

"Me!"

Granny waved her arms as though she were under attack by flies. "Quiet! Give me space. Back off."

The kids backed off.

"Okay," said Granny. "Here's how it is. I am not having a one-sex gang."

She glared at Bertie. "Boys are people."

She glared at Andy. "Girls are people."

She glared at them all. "Either everybody joins my gang — or nobody joins. We'll take a vote. Somebody bring me a watch."

Damaris dashed into the house and returned with a watch. Granny looked at it. "You have sixty seconds to decide." She snapped her fingers. "Begin."

Granny stepped away. She turned her back on them.

She waited. She could hear whispers. A squeak or two. Then silence.

At sixty seconds, she turned. Six faces staring. No smiles. No frowns.

What were they thinking?

She took a deep breath. "Here's the question. Everybody who wants to join my gang, raise your hand."

Six hands shot up.

Granny threw her arms in the air. "All riiiight! Looks like we got ourselves a gang!"

The kids mobbed her.

11

Two days later, Mrs. Pickwell was sorting sweaters in her thrift shop on Marshall Street. The doorbell jingled. In came Damaris and Bertie.

"Mom, can I join a gang?" said Damaris.

Mrs. Pickwell sighed. "I thought we went all over that."

"But this is a different gang, Mom. This one is better. This is a *good* gang."

"This is a *great* gang," added Bertie.

"Really?" said Mrs. Pickwell. "And what makes this gang so great?"

"Well, for one thing," said Bertie, "the captain."

Mrs. Pickwell grinned. "I suppose you mean yourself."

"Oh, no," said Bertie. "We have a new captain. One of the most respectable people in town. Probably in the *country*. Would you like to meet her?"

Mrs. Pickwell folded her arms. "I can hardly wait."

"Captain!" called Bertie. "You can come in now!"

When the captain walked through the doorway, Mrs. Pickwell nearly choked.

"Granny!"

"In the flesh," said the captain of the gang.

Mrs. Pickwell looked at Damaris.

"It's true, Mom. Granny is in charge. It's going to be the best gang ever. Can I join, Mom?"

Before Mrs. Pickwell could answer, Granny took her by the hand and led her outside.

The other members of the gang were standing around a pair of wagons. In the wagons were buckets of water, scrub brushes, soap, and piles of sponges.

"This will be the gang's main job," Granny explained. "They go around selling baths for pets. I got the idea when I saw Roscoe the duck at the Mud Hole the other day."

Granny faced the kids. "And who *are* we?"

The kids shouted as one: "The Bathwater Gang!"

"See, Mom?" pleaded Damaris. "Gangs *can* be good. Can I join now?"

Bertie unfolded a new copy of the gang's platform. She showed it to Damaris's mother. "This is what we stand for. You can tell it's all good stuff. Look at numbers nineteen, twenty, and twenty-one."

Mrs. Pickwell looked. She read out loud, "Peace. Love. Flowers." She burst out laughing. "Oh, all right — yes — yes."

The gang cheered.

Granny clapped her hands. "Okay, you guys. Off you go. You have work to do."

Bertie said, "Aren't you coming, Gran — uh, excuse me — Captain?"

"Oh, no," said Granny. "The captain doesn't work. The captain bosses. Now git!"

So off went the Bathwater Gang, in search of their first dirty dog . . . or crummy cat . . . or yucky ducky.